MEMOIRS OF SCHOOL

NEESHANT SRIVASTAVA

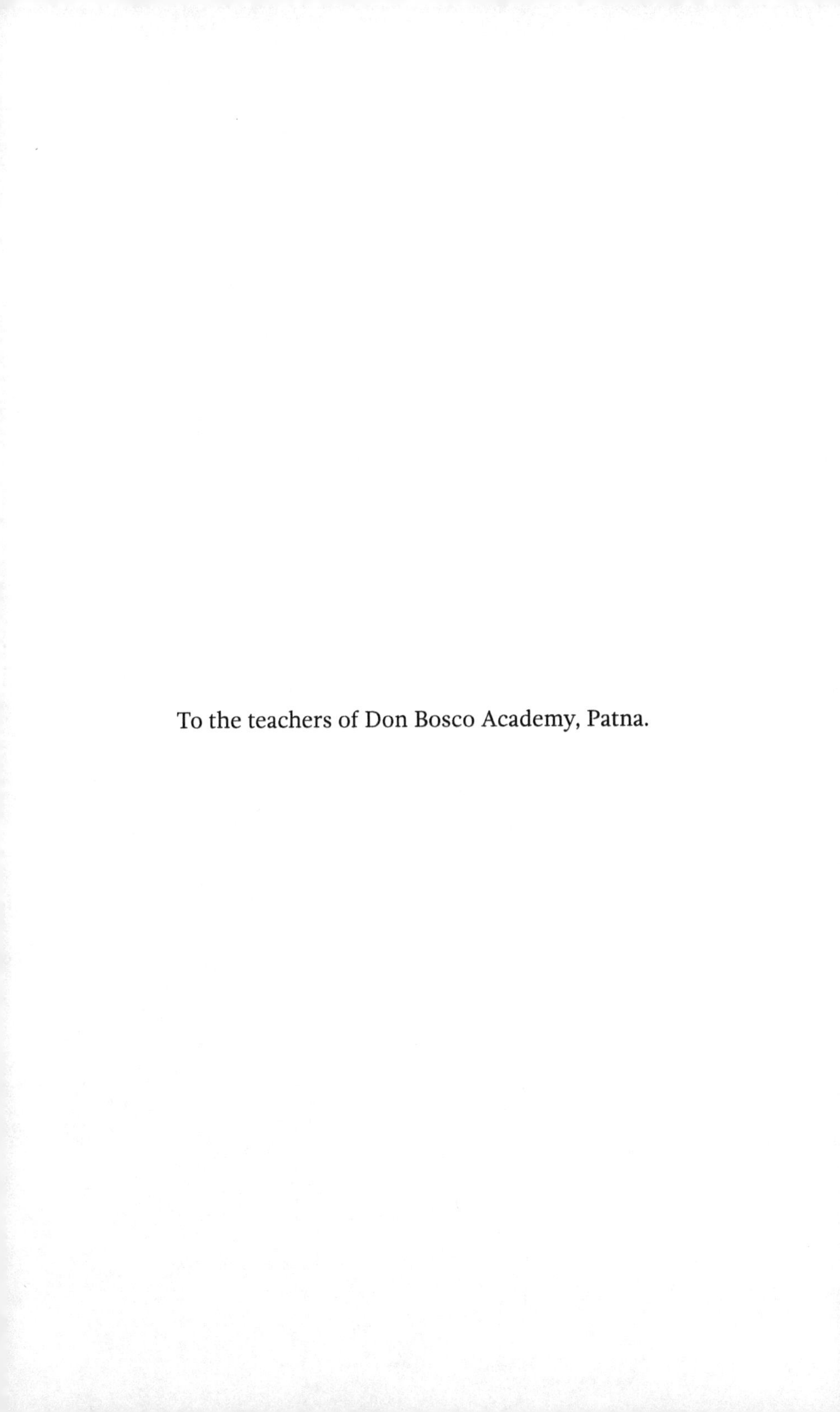

To the teachers of Don Bosco Academy, Patna.

Contents

CHAPTER ONE

THE PRINCIPAL AND HIS NASWAAR

I am the proud student of my alma mater, Don Bosco Academy, Patna, 1990 batch. Our principal, the respected, Mr. Alfred George deRozario was the founder of this school. The school started off with a few rented houses around the posh Pataliputra Colony, Patna and later on built its very own building, with a playground in Digha, Patna. It still carries on with great pride and is the shining jewel of Patna. It's beginning dates back to the year 1975-76 when it was more of a makeshift school.

I can never forget my school as it has made me the person I am today and the warmth and the hard work of its brilliant teachers still holds a special place in my heart. It makes me feel very privileged to be a part of the Don Bosco family. My education began at that school when we would jet in and jet out of cramped rooms and buildings that were worn out but still carried a strict discipline enforced by its many teachers. I joined Don Bosco Academy in the year 1987 when I was in the seventh standard. There was something about the school and its environment that made me forget about the lack of space for a free arm or leg swing. What we learnt within its premises was nothing short of excellence and I could feel the hard-working team of its teachers, trying to give something of value to its students. Life is too long, as they say, especially for children and we must spare a thought for them as they try to find a place in this world. Very often we hear the sad news of someone getting busted and their report card showing in red, the words, 'Failure'. I don't know if I passed in the game of life but I do remember a sweet gentleman by the name of Mr. Rozario and the way he treated us little children. I cannot forget his warmth when he happened to be on his 'rounds' of the classrooms. His smile and a gentle knock on our heads by his supreme sense of humour is hard to forget. He did make us smile as he left and his eyes carried the warmth and the sincerity that is hard to forget. Perhaps his signature note was the naswaar (tobacco snuff) and the characteristic hot nose as the tobacco got to him was quite evident. I cannot explain why I always carry the memories of the people I met long ago and many say that it is a useless exercise and I am just day dreaming. There is something in the eyes that takes me there and the world unfortunately has slowly drifted to an unknown place as I speak. Worthless bummers like me just sit in the corner and think about Mr. Rozario and his magnetism, a kind of romance if you would pardon me.

I heard that the principal, Mr. Rozario had built a Don Bosco hostel near the Golumber of Pataliputra Colony. It was filled with children from far off places and near that did not have a huge budget when it came to their children's education. Meagre canteen, food, rooms not far from dingy, darkness at the drop of the hat from power shedding that mainly occurred at night. I remember reading Julius Caesar in my tenth standard and watching a film of the same name in a small room somewhere in that hostel. While us children tried to figure out who was good and bad in that classic Shakespeare drama, our mouths were gorged with hot samosas and maybe some hot tea lasting barely enough for just over three sips, in a very small earthen kullhar. We heard how the principal's children played in the mud just at the entrance of the hostel and that were nothing more than some untidy street boys. Years pass too quickly and before we try to figure out this huge and mysterious life and try to harness it to our own good and advantage, time just races by and takes away the hair on our head. Well you would not believe that twenty seven years have just flown by and the hair has started to fall in the fifty year old that I have become. Now I am not sure where I want to go anymore but I think I think I should mention the last time that I visited my alma mater, Don Bosco Academy in its new building at Digha, Patna.

I don't remember why and how I had to visit my school again. All I know is that I took along my gardener, Mr. Baleshwar Das along with me to collect a certificate to show that I indeed has been a student of that school. I was very reluctant, I must say, for I didn't know who I might bump into, maybe the stylish and confident Mr. Donald Martin, my Physics teacher that gave it all with his preciseness and the beauty of his spoken words, a man for the hour, or Ms. Bedi, the spinster, our Chemistry teacher, and I am taking a grave risk in calling her that, and I am filled with a sense of speaking too much for my own good, and I wish and pray that Ms. Bedi then would have had a family of her own by now, Amen, or Mr. Arvind Shah, our History teacher and his famous words,

'This guy is good for nothing, and he will never do anything in life', to someone that stood up like shameless, when he was asked not to stand up over and over again with his nonsense questions and disrupt Mr. Shah's history class. Well, that guy did that in every class that we attended and he often popped up at my home and made a mess of my patience until finally time laid him to rest and let the good Lord bless him with happiness.

The above three teachers were pivotal in my life and I knew from the beginning that the above teachers never even noticed me when I was a child and attended their classes regularly, when Mr. Shah would sometimes hold my shoulder softly and offer a warm smile. God bless them all and I just did not want to face them on my last visit to my alma mater.

It was late afternoon when we reached the premises of the new building of Don Bosco Academy, Digha with Baleshwarji by my side. I walked in with total silence to see young children and classrooms with new sounds and everything else you would find in a normal school. My eyes were trying to hide and at the same time there was no danger at all, for the three teachers never knew who I was then and there was no possibility that they would know me now. Curiously I was taken straight to the office of the principal, the respected, Mr. Rozario. I saw him sitting at his chair, too old and still, and I promptly offered the typed document that I indeed had been a student of that school for the respected, Mr. Rozario's signature. I don't know why, something said that he had recognized me, although he never could have, for I had always been an invisible student throughout my three years at the prestigious, Don Bosco Academy. He signed and I left with Balaji at my side.

The story ends there and I never saw any of the three teachers at the new school at Digha. I inquired and they said that they had left the school a long time ago. I came back home, a little disappointed, for I could never forget the three people that changed the course of my life and I owe a great deal to those three teachers and the man who started it all, the respected, Mr. Rozario and his dream project of giving a sweet gift to little children that they may never forget that they were alive and happy for once in their lives.

CHAPTER TWO

VERSATILE MR. NASEEM AND HIS LUNA

I have had the privilege of having outstanding teachers at school and one of them was the good old Mr. Naseem. He taught Physics to students of higher standard of Don Bosco Academy, Patna, and I had to wait for three years to have the privilege of being his student. He was not a gaudy, showy personality and spoke very few words of English to make his outward appearance below the standard that was a hit among the students. He had a wiry body that could pass through the slightest of openings, be it a window or a door. He was mocked, too much for disbelief, for possessing the first pioneering transition from a bicycle called the luna. It did not possess powerful engines and one had to cycle fast enough to kick start the engine. I did not like it when someone passed a very hurtful comment against Mr. Naseem. I believe that a man is known for the simplicity that he wears and possesses and not by expensive accoutrements that he carries. The stone age was thus the age when there were real men and women, when to start a fire one had to wait for the rains to subside and the moistness and the wetness to disappear between two stones and the ingenuity to start a fire from a dying spark. A push button generation has only produced worthless generation of people that have nothing to do with nature, human feelings and the great sacrifice to set forth a life in motion.

I still remember Mr. Naseem and the stolidity of his face and the sheer disgust handling a bunch of worthless students that smirked too loud at his luna. For one Mr. Naseem in no way had any paucity of funds to buckle up in a bike of blinding speed, he just loved his luna. Our principal at that time, the respected Mr. Rozario was quite in tune with Mr. Naseem and valued his contributions in the field of Physics. I loved Mr. Naseem for the quiet disdain and a stern face that did not give a damn to what went around and never slackened his sense of purpose to drive the students that deserved to reach somewhere. I remember his eyes of stone, as he held a perpetual air of bland seriousness and on rare occasions a smile somehow slipped from his lips, that went unnoticed for he was an expert at hiding the goodies that could spread a sense of cheer and happiness. I don't know why I loved him and felt a certain connection that was hard to hide when eyes met. His warmth somehow seeped in through his eyes and the softening of his lips after some harsh words for the heathen. We did not feel much strength in his classes and the common word that he was nothing but an ordinary teacher. But just when things were settled and done with, he uttered something that hit the very meat of the matter and those that had the ear to hear the final words found it most outstanding. He was a versatile teacher and echoed the general sentiment throughout his classes that was most disgusting and made him appear like a frustrated man. He spoke very little about the real subject and that too at lightening speed and was gone before the boys could gather anything. His main agenda was to correct the falling majority and teaching them what really mattered in life. Education is certainly useless, the real thing is how one treats other people, how much respect do we have for the teacher. Is he below the level of the students and the students above the level of the teacher. If at all such a day arrives then it is just the beginning of the end for the student in question. The real education that we call 'Vidya' in Hindi is respect for the 'guru' or the teacher. Do not go to the teacher to learn the finer points of trigonometry or the cryptic logic to get at the final answer and excel in the exam hall. You are only fooling yourself, for we are the children of God. And God it is that created us and this world and for your quick perusal, the human mind, if you should know. One invisible switch turned off will be the end of the brain, the most sort after engine of arrogance. Hence when in front of a teacher in a class, behave like the loyal cadet in front of sergeant trainer that must say 'yes' to everything, even if the trainer goes wrong and says something that is blatantly incorrect. Maybe the sergeant has something on his mind and is just playing the fool to test the cadet. A teacher in Hindu culture is called a 'guru' and which again in Hindu culture is higher that God Himself. And God Almighty, my friend, don't even begin to say something about Him, its much more than a cardinal sin. Teachers, like parents, know more than children can ever know in a lifetime. Bow before the Guru, do not speak, but listen.

The second and the last occasion that I had the chance to meet Mr. Naseem, and this time personally was when he suggested that I should take tuitions from him. There was one more student that was to join Mr. Naseem in his tuitions and that one was a brat, a roadside troublemaker and too difficult to reform. I do not remember much what I studied and the length of the tuition class, I somewhat remember the place and the image of the boy that was certainly wasting his time.

I had an abrupt end to the tuition classes and I somehow cannot recollect what exactly was the focus of my studies – was it Newton's Laws, gravity principle, Archimedes Principle, the study of the celestial bodies out there in space, the principle of action and reaction, velocity principles or some other jewel of Physics which Mr. Naseem had mastered. Mr. Naseem sat back and spoke a few words softly that somehow blinded the student who somehow focussed on his resplendent and calm face with eyes like diamonds to hypnotise the student and make him forget everything. It all boiled down to the obvious conclusion that Mr. Naseem was ill equipped to teach the subject of Physics. He just let it go with 'aye

aye' and 'A men...', and his throw of words that brought out the devil in the boys as they loved the signing off that spoke of his uncaring attitude and inertness to the colossal mess floating around.

I never saw Mr. Naseem ever again and time, the great eraser of memory let Mr. Nassem dwindle in my mind and being blurry is not even close to the damage done as people of the past and those moments sink into the black abyss and be lost forever. Fair enough then I have had to create moments in my mind but like divine power whatever I did conjure was just about what happened, albeit a few aberrations. Such is life and the famous Beatles song, 'There are places I remember...' aptly describes what those lost roads, people and events were all about and what they mean to us. In a fairly long life, the adult stage puts us in an air tight shoe box where there is no light and any hope of reviving the past is almost impossible. There are people that came into our lives when we were young and even when we were children and touched us by doing something that was sweet, like a glowing smile, and left us forever and we got busy in collecting lifeless things that did not mean anything and we did go too far, never to find our way back again. This is the sad chapter of humanity and God always lends everybody with a complete mind and body and a potential to experience the magic that is life and we get too busy in finding our way in closed rooms with no fresh air and the body simply crumbles and the mind goes dead. Mr. Naseem was an exciting chapter in my life and I can just look at his eyes and feel the magic that comes with complete peace of mind. It is then that we return to innocence as we debate over very little things and the people around us, especially women, just have a laugh and utter from sweet lips,

'O! poor baby'.

The difference in this innocence and the 'obvious' innocence is the depth of thought when we can write a book of philosophy over a simple thing as – 'one plus one is two.'

Goodbye Mr. Naseem, and all those teachers that taught me and were gracious enough to point out my mistake and punish me severely for incomplete homework or something as queer as not wearing the right shade of overcoat (%$#@!!!).

CHAPTER THREE

THE CHEMISTRY TEACHER - THE SPINSTER Ms. BEDI

I first saw her in my tenth standard. She was a Chemistry teacher of Don Bosco Academy, Patna. She was initially just one of our teachers, but later on she became our class teacher. She was young, heavy, and carried a kind of dismissive air, a pride proud in her eyes, and words that echoed around many walls when she spoke. She was a no-nonsense woman when it came to handling a bunch of awkward boys of the class and plenty of bitter remarks flung at no one's mercy, always. Sometimes in a huddle of students we often said she was a 'frustrated' young woman, and a whisper that no one could hear of her being a spinster. She did not look like the marrying kind, given her weight and features that were more masculine than feminine. We genuinely cared for her for she was a brilliant teacher, a great speaker, motivator with a deep knowledge of Chemistry. She talked as if she didn't care what happened to her, her fingers all white as if she were a mason and her dress spoke of her death rather than a woman growing younger with age, like most women do. Her words always hurt the students and everyday at school was like the final ultimatum to us students that very soon we shall face total annihilation, and a fiasco that would haunt us the rest of our lives, a little short of us being juvenile delinquents, I guess. Ms. Bedi was especially hard on 'mediocre' students, and I have always been a living example of that group. She backed boys that were toppers and near the top rankers of the class and school. In my entire life at school, I could never ever understand or even try to understand these geniuses, such knowledge and the perfection and the intelligence that goes with it. I can vouch for the fact that there are more mediocre in this world than toppers. These set of people suffer so much that one day they forget the fact that they are 'human'. But I firmly believe in one thing and I am speaking from experience of forty-seven years, that a truly 'successful' person is one that has always failed in life, but has the courage to stoke the ship in high waters and never give up. 'Success' is the greatest failure. And from experience again I can say, and if at all I can be pardoned, that these great 'toppers' did not do so well in life. Life is not a spark but a constant flame and it needs great courage to produce such a flame and only God can 'grant' such a flame, if at all, and it is never about the final marks that a student gets in his examination, for examinations are phony for a certain tactful ploy is all that is required to get good marks. That is, let me be pardoned again, is 'cheating', cheating life itself. Let me again tell you, and I am surely running out of pardons, if someone cheats life, then I am afraid life is just one colour, the colour of lust.

Ms. Bedi, and I just could not understand why I always failed before her, and the Teacher's pet was some bright student and Ms. Bedi would cup-hand the back of the head of the pet. I had had the experience of getting her attention on just two occasions. One was when I wrote in a terminal exam of History. She was then the class teacher and I caught her attention just once. It so happened that when I was busy writing the history paper, I somehow misread the watch and thought that there was just thirty minutes left for me to complete my paper and answer all the required number of questions. I hurried up and finished writing the entire paper in about twenty minutes. My hand writing was horrible and when I realized that there was one more hour left to complete the paper,

I just could not do anything about it. I just sat there thinking that I was bound to be reprimanded by higher authority, or maybe not. There are times when we get away with the crime that we have committed. I thought that there was nothing wrong in that, given that it was not my fault, although it was my fault. I believe that I am that unlucky student that never missed the cane of the teacher for a crime that I indeed had committed. Just so, I was called by Ms Bedi, or rather plucked from the class when she was discussing our performance in the terminal examination, she was the class teacher, if you remember.

"How horrible Neeshant, is this the way you write your exam paper, your handwriting is so bad. I will not accept this, please sit down."

The second and the last occasion that I faced Ms. Bedi was during the PTA meeting. My father walked with me to the school, and no words were exchanged. There were many times like this one when I walked with my father, or travelled with my father and the only thing heard was the noise around, the sound of his footsteps and if we were on a train the swinging symphony and the lovely sound of the train running lazily along the tracks. The people around just added to the mayhem and there was not getting away from it.

We reached our classroom and Ms. Bedi was busy as usual, swinging her arms and giving the 'eye' to the student in question, while gently conversing with the parents. Her words were always bitter and I wonder if she had any 'womanlike' qualities and I would surely have been caned severely for what I just said. But I shall take the hurt, like I always have. Our turn came and Ms. Bedi was ready with her gun. She acted as if there was no hope for me in the world, she was so harsh that my father simply shook his head with nothing to say at all.

"This is the pre-board exams sir, and his aggregate percentage is way down low and I am not bringing other student's performance into picture, if you will. Sir, if he does not show any improvement then I am afraid he will not get admission anywhere after tenth and the road is always downhill, severely downhill after that. I think I have made my point clear, thank you very much for coming."

This was the last time that I saw Ms. Bedi or even heard from her. 'Brilliant' students often dropped at her home for a cup of tea, perhaps, and Ms. Bedi always obliged. She was very clear about her thinking and that was that 'mediocrity' is a disease and in this competitive world it is the marks that survive and diseased people are bound to be slaughtered in this cruel world. She was very right I must say and later on in life I dragged my feet into the ground to just about survive, and my marks like always were awful. You would be astounded when I tell you that there is a reason for 'mediocrity' and every student that relates to that group of people is not in any way inferior to the most intelligent and scripted geniuses. I need not point out the reason for mediocrity, it's as clear as a bright sunny day, those that know, know what I am talking about.

As for me, I was never the giving up kind. If scoring 97% in Biology paper is because the question paper was too easy, then I am fooling myself. I got admission in 10+2 in St. Michael's High School, Patna by merit and I have never struggled getting admission in good colleges on merit.

As for Ms. Bedi, she was a jewel in the crown. A lady completely dedicated to her work and ready to sacrifice herself at the cost of being called a 'spinster'. I have had many teachers in school, and I fondly remember a few ladies that happened to be my class teachers too.

Wherever she is right now, I know that God must have blessed her with all the happiness in the world. I have never seen an 'iron' woman like Ms. Bedi. I thank her for being a strong force in my life and giving me words that pushed me to greater heights in getting the gift of 'education'.

CHAPTER FOUR

DEBATE COMPETITION

It's one of the great achievements of students, young and old, to participate in a debate competition. It is a test of one's ability to put forward one's side, point of view, and being bold enough to face defeat or a simple mockery of what someone said. It is hard to take sides when everything has logic behind it and justifies even the most obvious dirty act put in words. The greatest thing that a debater has, which he prides and because of which he has a sense of arrogance about him, is confidence, big enough to say something. Confidence is great to have and most often than not a child is brought up in a way that he holds confidence as he goes along. He is praised for even the silliest thing he says or does. He is called the 'greatest' that the world has seen even if it is not true by any standards. By the time he reaches college, this boy (and I am not avoiding girls here) has developed a natural confidence and can anytime look you in the eye or the eye of the person he is addressing in a debate and rock the crowd with a loud thunder (the way Elvis did, in his confident moves). This guy can never go wrong, believe me, and so has he been told throughout his life. But we must all remember that language has a boundary and we must be awake enough to respect that boundary. Please don't say anything and get away with it. Why then do we have libels and slander all over the papers and videos. I have heard people saying things that are 'bad' and too 'dirty' to be uttered and especially for people that have a good character. That's how the story goes.

I was afraid of debates and for that reason it is no surprise that in my entire life I have participated in just one debate, at the school level, a long time ago. I don't know how I gathered the courage to participate in that debate, for I have been the most under confident child, if not at present. I was scared to utter a word, lest it may hurt someone or be of a great dishonour to someone's pride and respect gathered over a lifetime. I am the kind of child that was brought up by a father who never took us to the moon (my elder brother and me), or said things that every child wants to hear. We were scared of opening our mouth, even without the presence of my father. When we were with our father, we could not dare even whisper. We had suffered for the crime of opening our mouths, which uttered words out of place, or somehow did not go well with my father and very often were damaging, perhaps, in some way. The damage could be directly to my father or mother or some distant person that was not a part of our lives in any way. And hence we never had the confidence that a person is naturally brought up with. Confident people appear to be saints, like they have unearthed a rare phenomenon.

I was in the ninth grade. There was a boy called Arup in our class. He was making a list of students that could be a part of his group in a team to participate in a debate competition with him as the leader. He went about selecting students randomly and I know don't know how and when his eyes fell on me. He said,

"Neeshant, I like you to be a part of my group and participate in the upcoming interclass debate competition."

I looked around, not sure if he was talking to me. I had always been the last man in the queue of aspiring students. I could not utter my name properly, speaking in front of students would be a comic spectacle, I was sure. But I gathered my nerve and was very excited to say the least. Arup was giving out topics and I happened to catch one that slipped out of his lips and caught my fancy. I do not remember what the topic was, my memory cannot go so far back and then there are things that God wants us to forget. There were about three in my group (even that is a guess, but I think it is close) and the one leader, Arup was to speak at the end. I was to speak as the second speaker and Arup just touched my shoulder and nodded. I went home and started preparing my script for the debate to be conducted in about a weeks' time. I wish I could tell you what the topic was, that would have made the story even more interesting.

It was like the festive season in our school. Boys, and only boys, were busy with their colour pens, charts of assorted colours, water colours, sketch pens and of course their creative mind that would steal the imagination of the people around. There were painting competitions, speeches, debates, sports, musical chairs, dumb charades, to commemorate the annual day of the school. I was getting nervous sitting at home, imagining the day that was a week away, with me not knowing what to say, and people just staring at me, and I don't know why, as if I were some kind of clown or I had made some grave error somewhere that was hard to erase. The great stage fright always managed to empty the performer of everything, including and most importantly his words. I never counted myself among those people that spoke so fluently and passionately, without any break or flinch, as if they were in their living rooms, talking with so much ease. Among such people stood our leader, the great Arup. He stood before the crowd and spoke as if he were licking the cream off a softy in an ice cream parlour, so confident, so smooth and I have to add the missing word, 'flamboyance'.

The big day came. Among all the frills and sagging of festoons, glitter touching the ground, maybe wet by a puddle somewhere, and students and teachers in the last remains of a grand festival, winding up in a few days and the debate like the penultimate thing to happen. It was afternoon, I think, and all were stout with lavish lunches in tight tiffin and the occasional burp heard here and there, like the whole community were dozing off. And then four of us were required to stand straight and push our eyes wide, and call forth some adrenalin, so late in the day, to add some spark to a sleepy afternoon. The audience had gathered in a small classroom, too many to come in one small room and someone by the name of Mrs. Morrison.

She was an old lady, I heard the investor and friend of the principal, and naturally very rich, in some island, I cannot state the exact facts about her, we lived on rumours and the reality was hidden deep somewhere. She was an elegant lady to say the least, looked like an English woman, carrying the customary etiquette of the English people and the rare grace that an Englishman/woman carries. I have never been to England, but we get to know a lot about the people over there, and it is no surprise. She had a pleasant smile and was sitting on the benches among the students, she was not all that tall, not far from the speaker. Without delay, the first speaker was called and he did all that he could, followed closely by the second. I was the third and didn't want my name to be called out, I was too shy. But the big moment came and I gathered all that I had, and precisely nothing at all, and stood in front of silly little children, who were too small to elicit any seriousness. They were more interested in the weather outside, the free-flowing green leaves, casually in the soft breeze and the bright light of the sun, rather than being stomped in some kind of aching burrow.

I stood there before the big eyes of Mrs. Morrison and began my speech, or was it some kind of a prejudice, so typical of a debate. The first few lines were the greetings and no one ever took it seriously, for it was sheer flattery with no truth in it.

"Respected..."

A few lines into my speech, and I forgot my words to allow sweat to illustrate the scarcity of the virtues of a confident person. I looked down, luckily, I had the script in my hand, which I carried, just in case. I read out what was written on the paper, and again looked down, and again looked down, until finally I took the entire matter into my hands and the whole crowd laughed and giggled. I noticed that first time I looked into the paper for some help, Mrs. Morrison had a sweet smile on her face, followed by some nodding of the head, that was hard to notice. It was a day of great shame for me and I just completed my misery only to hear the audience clap and clap and hoot. I have never forgotten Mrs. Morrison's look on her face, and her sweet smile, as if to tell me that it was all good. Long live Mrs. Morrison.

Arup was his usual and the crowd just melted into his words, the perfectionist. That day I was very happy and Arup too was happy. He smiled at me and said,

"Good work, well done."

At the end of it all I earned the first ever certificate of my life,

"Master so and so...participated in the interclass debate...and..." I cannot remember all the words, and I do have that certificate somewhere deep in my trunk and I last looked at it some...ago, I can't say. It was a proud moment for me and later on in my life I never ever participated in any debate competition, be it High school or college, or anywhere else. I happen to join a Toastmaster's club many years later where people come and speak on the podium and I just sat in the audience wondering when my chance would come to hold the podium and say something. I was made a defunct treasurer of the Toastmaster's club and sometimes I was called on the podium to invite someone on the stage. I remember, though, I did finally got a chance to speak and in my sickness (I had developed a sickness of the mind), I said a few words turning my head like on the pivot to reach the eye of each gazer, and everybody staring at me, like they could make out what I was saying and I did find some faces disgusted to see me there and gave smashed faces, like I were most uninvited and was no more than a lunatic.

I can stand in front of an audience today, but I can tell you that I have nothing to say. What I have learnt in my life is through poverty, not just what it naturally means, but poverty graver than any poverty ever known, and that is the poverty of the spirit. How can I live in a world and enjoy the fun floating around when there have been millions of people, including my dear father and mother that have shred their hearts to the bone, in trying to bring some justice to the immense suffering that men and women have been through, it's heart wrenching, its too sad, and the man that walks aloof is the poorest that will ever be. It's time that we all should sit down and take notice of those people that were too busy to feel the tears of each passing generation of people, that burned and burned just for a good life for their children. After all we are all humans, and not some cattle or sheep. A tear of love is all we have to give to those brave men or women.

CHAPTER FIVE

MY MEDIOCRE FRIENDS

'Friends are like poison, or the limiting force in anyone's life. Yet they can be uplifting too.'

The above lines do not come from some great philosopher, I have not quoted anyone. It comes from my own experience of the wonderful friends I had throughout my life. A flash in the pan on a sunny day is enough to attract a friend into one's life. Yet it is said that true friends are hard to come by, just like true love, that has almost disappeared from the world. Yes, I have had friends before, just like sweethearts in a school teenage ball. Oh! How wonderful, me and my girl hand in hand and her face resting on my shoulders and some romantic song playing in the background, I can almost fall in love right now. But I am not talking about girls here, but pure hot-blooded boys, in an all-boys school. The above was just a dream for I never came to the proximity of a girl.

My friendship started when I was in my shorts, as far as I can remember and my first good friend was someone by the name of V. Bharat. I never knew what the 'V' stood for and I never asked him. He was as black as me, but there was something in his eyes, and the softness that he exuded. We studied in the same class and walked together during lunch time. We belonged to the 'mediocre' club and try hard as we may, our overall percentage in exams never crossed the infamous 'sixty' river. Sometimes it fell below sixty and to tell you the truth, at its very best, it reached the early sixties. Yet I was happy, my friend V. Bharat was happy, my father was happy, and my mother just did not care, she just smiled and played around with my fluffy cheeks. I cannot exactly remember our talks or discussions, if it ever went that deep, but all I know that I loved him and he loved me. We walked together for less than a year, when I was studying in a school in New Delhi, where my father was posted, and then just like the Fall, we parted without a sound. That was the end of my first true friendship. He never inquired where I went and what I did after our parting, and neither did I. I hope he is a happy fifty-year-old, somewhere, and doubt that he ever thinks about me just like I do. My real friendship 'group' started when we landed in Patna, after my father took retirement, in a popular school of those times, Don Bosco Academy. We formed a strong group of friends, again the infamous 'mediocre' group, and were rather proud of it. This is the story, or a short sketch, if you will, of the three years I spent in the school, from the seventh grade to the tenth grade. We had the same book in – Physics, Biology, Chemistry to be followed for three years and just like their wear and tear by constant use and 'over' use our friendship too blossomed in a not so pleasant environment. I am not talking about the dearth of proper infrastructure of the school, or the lack of supplies of things like stationery or school uniform which did hit our group, but what went around us, the way teachers treated our group of friends and the way we were looked down upon by other 'geniuses' of the school. In spite of the poverty, our friendship remained firm and it is very sad that our friendship got lost in the tides of time when each individual, especially boys that become men, have to prove their worth and lose a great thing in the process. That thing is called 'life' and the beautiful thing called the 'self' which has to be dug out with great force from the trenches or the deep coal mines. Money and its strength are not the final destination and an effort to amass riches leave us 'poor' within.

Let me tell you a little about our group. Primarily the group was made up of three friends – Chinmay Chandan, Manish Mittal and me. We can always add a few more that came and went but the above three remained together throughout. The very first person to impress me the most was Chinmay Chandan. He was a tall guy, taller than me back then and I was particularly touched by the way he struggled with not enough money and very little to say by way of defence or claim something big. Words hardly came out of his lips and that was a remarkable thing. He wore a crumpled shirt that always ran short of crease, forcing him to pull the fold left after a deep tuck to straighten it and give some kind of dignity. His shoes were worn out and always carried a hole, which was cleverly hidden too. He wore glasses just like me, even before I started wearing them and he constantly adjusted them for it was too old and loose for him, with a constant finger to push it back to the nose bridge. A smart boy with short hair and a constant smile, somehow. He called out my name in whichever way he could and the silence that surrounded this boy, in spite of his struggles was indeed touching. I loved him very much. Sad to say that one day Chinmay, after we got out of school and completed our intermediate, came to my home. I was surprised for he lived far away, about fifteen kilometres away. He looked happy that day and as he sank into a chair and my hands ready with a cup of tea that my mother prepared, he said,

"I've got admission in BIT Mesra."

probably, in the Electronics branch, if I remember correctly, well I am just guessing.

"There are huge tennis courts..."

It is difficult to quote exactly what he said. I guess he said a lot more but I cannot recall it completely. There was happiness in his eyes, and it really made me happy. I was happy for a boy that struggled so hard at school. I saw him off and he was on his way.

That same year I got admission in Bihar College of Engineering, Patna, in the Mechanical branch. What I am about to tell you now is heartbreaking and I just could not believe my eyes or the fact that we were once good friends. I was walking to the gates of my college one day, and I saw Chinmay walking by, he lived in the nearby area, about fifteen kilometres from my house. I looked at him expecting love to give in anytime and make us smile together and maybe take a walk. I was astonished when Chinmay never looked at me and walked straight. I tried to jog my memory if he was the same guy. How could I forget the face of my dearest friend, and the days we had spent in school in bad times and good times. The love we shared was hard to forget and I learnt a lesson or two from him. I stopped in my steps and looked at him passing by, as if I were a nonentity. I just carried on and never lost the place I had for him in my heart. Years later I happened to work in Bangalore in some IT company. I heard about Chinmay through 'social networking', that was an infant back then. He had become the Manager of Oracle, IT database company. I was happy to see him (in a picture) after a long time but never tried to contact him, for I was nothing as compared to him, his status. I was also happy for the man that struggled very hard and 'poverty' was the rule back in those days. The story ended there and I hope he is happy now. My second friend like I mentioned was by the name of Manish Mittal. He was the son of a rich businessman. He had a lot of things, and I know that you know what I am talking about. I did not talk to him much and he too had strong connections with Chinmay. Well, he went his way in life and I heard that he has a very successful training centre in Gujarat. Life in general is a three-step process after school – college, job and marriage. In the process we lose friends, make new friends and the parents should know how to take care of themselves.

My 'mediocre' friends did well in life and the students that were toppers in our school, that the teachers adored did even better.

I do not want to mention the friends I made after the tenth grade, at the intermediate level in a popular school in Patna by the name of St. Michael's High School. The reason for my exclusion is that the friends I made after the tenth grade were far from 'mediocre', they were a class apart. They were too good, to say the least and almost all the students that came out of St. Michael's High School in the year 1992 became world renowned, or at least known in our country. The list is endless and the huge class of 1992, with almost sixty students could not be counted on my fingers.

But I always miss my 'mediocre' group that I had at Don Bosco Academy. Mediocrity is not meant to include those that were kind of 'slow' brain or incompetent. There is nothing like 'mediocrity', if you ask me. I loved that class because of the small things we valued back then. It could be a small glass of hot tea for Rs.2/- or one hot samosa for Rs. 3/-. It could be a small pencil that was used until it did not fit between fingers, but somehow gave service until its last breath. This is the story of small things that really matter, like camaraderie, service, friendship, love. This is a small moment of standing under the shade of a tree, with its huge leaves, to give a cold whiff of breeze in the hot sun. This is a journey, my friend, a lifelong journey. I am happy to report that there are men and women in this world and always will be, that have made the journey through hard times and endless strife, the confusion that burns in everyone's brain all the time, like we are one among a swarm of flies that erupts every time it senses the sound of a mindless swat. This is an exclusive club, my friend. Ask those that burnt for others, that spent their whole life in service, without knowing what was going on or what their own dreams were. Life is a delicate matter, and they say that a small spill from a water vessel carried on the head while walking, can end it. Don't let your goal in life be to fatten your purse, my friend, when all we need is a few rupees for a warm cup of tea on a pleasant evening.

CHAPTER SIX

MATHEMATICS AND MISERY

Name the greatest mathematician of India- the great Srinivasa Ramanujan. If mathematics were poetry, then the above was the greatest poet ever. To everyone's surprise mathematics to him was indeed like poetry to a miserable poet. Mathematics is the root cause of Hollywood or Bollywood. There were people that shunned this subject, were called worthless objects, like some burden on this earth, until they brought about a revolution, to change the thinking of people. They declared that there were greater things on this planet than numbers and the only mathematics required to live a beautiful life is in the simple logic- that one and one make two.

I come from a country (India) where Mathematics is an essential subject. Deep down in Bihar, where my roots lie, this subject is as simple as a young boy's crush on a girl in school or college. It is as simple as a cup of tea in the morning, or like a song that is hummed without any purpose. I know of a friend of mine in school by the name of Piyush. We studied together in the eighth or nineth grade, it's hard to remember which. This was a poor boy that lived in a boy's hostel. I liked him because of his smile and a simple and caring attitude towards me. It was a record that this boy never scored less than ninety prevent in Mathematics, I guess always, at least I saw it when we studied together. Like I said this was a poor boy, not to say that my family was filthy rich, my father was on pension of rupees ten thousand and our family of four barely survived on that money. This boy, I guess did not have even that luxury. Why would he be in a boarding school, that was not very expensive. It held poor boys like him that sometimes did not have enough money to pay the boarding school charges. I will explain that even further and you would be astonished with what I am going to tell you, and maybe you won't quite believe what I am going to tell you. No more secrets. This boy had enough money to buy one notebook for the entire year, yes you heard me, one small thin notebook for the entire year. He did all his roughwork, calculations and carried notes of other subjects in just this one notebook. Maybe I am exaggerating it a wee bit. But I can tell you that this boy practised Maths on this one notebook. When the notebook was full, he turned back the pages to the first page and wrote on the little blank spaces that were left after filling in the notebook once, and did all his Mathematics calculations. He wrote and rewrote but never gave up, always finding enough space to do rough work and practice his Mathematics. Like I said that this boy never scored less than ninety percent in Mathematics, always, be it terminal exams or the final exams. He was such a humble boy and such a star in Mathematics, teachers knew and the boys knew and had great respect for him. This is Bihar, and how geniuses exist in every nook and cranny and how they have struggled and still struggle with little no money at all. I call him a genius and a very warm person to be with. Mathematics was something I did not detest, but I was never good at it. More than the problem or the question, the sound of it put my mind in a tizzy. Mathematics meant an immediate answer on the lips, after all it is nothing but logic. For a person that used his heart more than his mind, it was an impossible puzzle of life to tackle and solve. I can tell you, in come the mathematics teacher in the class, of course all stood up with a 'Good morning, Sir', followed by unpleasant sound of children taking their seats without anyone speaking a word. The moment the teacher opened the mathematics book and turned the pages to where he had left off the previous day, all eyes were on him. He took out a problem and asked the class to turn the pages. People like me and me of course took refuge in the back of the person sitting in front of us, and hid our faces. He started writing on the blackboard with his back towards the class, broke the problem into smaller chunks, easy to swallow and starting yelling out the problem within a problem for a swift and quick reply. There were always these brilliant boys scattered around the class, including the back benchers that looked like those lofty men that had cracked the code with an up-collar bullying zest. An answer was always ready to wet the lips of our geniuses of the class. Sometimes, however, a question went straight through and passed through the facing wall of the class without any interruption and it was then that the teacher turned his head around, which had been nailed to the back board till then and jogged his eyeballs to find a face that would know the answer, with a final, 'Anyone'. If there was no one at all, he looked around for someone that had been sleeping in the classroom all this while, but the fact being that those that were sleeping were in fact shaking and trembling in a corner like a scared rabbit trying to avoid the penetrating eyes of the teacher. He then got angry and threw his chalk to someone at random for an answer. He was then not looking for an answer at all, as he shut the damn book and threw it on the table placed near the blackboard, and poured his frustrations of his life on the innocent boys,

"You rascals, we work so hard for you, and all you do is sleep in the class. I am trying to concentrate and work hard with you. All you do is come here, sit on your asses and have a merry time. Good for nothing people."

By this time the back benchers had straightened their collars and one of them got up, as if he had felt the struggle of the teachers and held the invisible spirit of the hard-working teachers, as if he were the representative of the class and the rest were his followers.

"Sir, I like to apologize on behalf of the class. We care for you and the hard work that you put in each day. It's just that the problem was too tough for us to crack it. We are extremely sorry, Sir."

By now the anger on the face of the teacher had disappeared and then the infamous bell rang and the class was in total disarray, as if there were no teacher in the class. They shouted and shouted more like in a fish market and walked out of the class before the teacher could gather his things. It is a record that I never faced the chalk pellet in my entire school career, never with any teacher. I am lucky indeed, for I was one of those scared rabbits that I talked about earlier.

Like I said that the problem with Mathematics is not Mathematics itself but just the time given to reach an answer, the time given to bring forth the result, which is in my view is very less. There are cheaters in this world that will tell you what one and one is, like they invented the result. It's on their lips, somehow, to show that they are good in the subject. It is in fact a confidence booster, for I can't tell you how a little boys feel when they just lip the answer at the stroke of a question. Others are rejected as 'weak' in Mathematics. This realization dawned in me very late, too late to convince my father that my mind could do the calculations, albeit taking its own time. For I remember that disastrous morning very well, and one that I shall carry to my death bed. I was in the seventh or eighth grade and my elder brother was in the tenth grade. It was a normal day and as usual our family of four gathered for lunch at our beautiful dining table. My mother never ate with the men and the boys. It was a tradition and I can tell you that she followed it till the last day of her life. There were three of us at the table, then, my father at on edge, where the head of the house sits, and my brother and me at either ends of the long sides of the table. I was always a hungry baby, and food was like a life saver for me. It was because of my love for food that I had developed a pot belly too early in my life. But let's not divert from the meat of the matter, here. My father asked me a mathematics question and I just stopped that wet morsel halfway into my mouth. I looked at my father, right into his eyes. He softly repeated the question, and I was moved to tears which grew into a weep, a cry and a final attempt to leave the table with unfinished food.

"Sit down, did I ask you to leave." My father wanted to kill me that day.

He turned his gaze to my elder brother,

"Any guesses."

My brother, the living genius, who didn't quite like what he ate, voiced the answer casually like he had the brain of a computer. My father looked at me and pulled me back to my seat, holding my arms tightly as I tried to run away and dive into a pillow.

"You are too weak, my son. If you can't answer this simple question then God save you."

My mother heard my crying and she shut off the gas and came ranting at my father,

"Is this the way you treat your children, shame on you."

He then let me go and my mother, the kind woman, like always, came to me and held the back of my head, softly,

"You don't worry, son. Your father is a bad man. A good for nothing man, I must say, here..."

I cried and cried, and tears had always been my best friend, they never failed to make me feel better.

It was out on the streets and everywhere, that I was weak in Mathematics. My uncles were pressed into service and holding the thick bad book they tried to break the monster into small chunks for me to follow. I could follow, if I were left alone and in peace. From thereon I did not score much in Mathematics and all my uncle's efforts were in vain. It came to the point of my tenth board exams. My class teacher, Ms. Bedi, called my father to school in PTA meeting. I walked along with my father to school, hoping that my class teacher would have at the most a good word for me, not knowing the results of the pre-board exams which were to be declared that day, with the yellow alarm in the hard hands of Ms. Bedi. The school was abuzz with noise of the children, their parents, some screaming out of joy and some out of defeat, and some chit-chat that was the usual thing, anywhere. We walked to my classroom and there was Ms. Bedi, ready with her gun, red lips that were meant for sweeter things than to give out warnings and a dash of death with a sweet perfume adding to the paradox.

"Here, Mr. Srivastava, right. Let me pull out the report card of Neeshant, Ah! Here it is.

OK, Sir I had warned you earlier and I am warning you again that your son has shown no improvement in any subject at all, barring a few. And Mathematics, Sir, what is the problem with you Neeshant. With such poor marks in Mathematics, your son is doomed. I am afraid there is no hope at all for him, not that there was any hope earlier. Sir, I have seen lives getting destroyed and young children taking to the streets and doing drugs. If this boy does not do well in the upcoming board exams, then God save your child. And Neeshant this History paper, what have you done. The History teacher was complaining when he saw your paper, what horrendous handwriting, most unintelligible. Is this the way you write your paper. Were you in some kind of hurry, like to catch the evening train to Allahabad. Son, tighten up or else, you just forget it, life is not meant for people like you. Sir, I hope, I am not being rude."

My father just nodded his head, did not utter a word. He picked up the report card and we walked home with the only sound to be heard was that of our footsteps and perhaps the random rush of the wind.

I reached home and my father wanted to forget the episode by a strong cup of hot tea that my mother had prepared and then a gentle walk to his bed, followed by a long sleep.

I had probably heard from my father, by his reaction,

"Just do what you can and let the rest go free out of the window."

If I know anything at all in a long hard life, is to struggle and never give up. I have found more of the darkness that light and my efforts have somehow failed miserably. Yet I walk and I walk and that's all I know.

I came home disappointed. I thought I had not worked hard enough. I always found a way to blame myself for everything, especially when I failed in the eyes of the other. I took out my books, that old tattered ones which had become too dull by the number of times I had flipped its pages. I immersed myself in books when the board exams were a few months away. I read those dull and complete logic that seemed to me to stand on a weak foundation or the kind of foundations that was hidden behind some kind of veil and not revealed to mediocre students like me. It all sounded great and perfect in the end, as if the conclusion was a written law that no one could ever doubt. I spent too much time on the way that tree of logic came to be when I was required to fasten the end to my memory and let in loose in the exams. In other words the conclusion were more important and needed to be learned by rote without much ado about the process of getting there. I have always doubted this method of learning and many a times been mocked for going too deep into the matter, instead of learning how to deliver the goods in the exam hall and jump to the road of success. This is perhaps the reason why I have failed more than I have succeeded. A glaring example of this failure is the IIT JEE exams in which I appeared three times- 1992,1993,1994 and with no surprise, I never qualified. Let's no go too far into those losses, I must come back to my tenth board exams. I studied during the day, I studied during the night, I studied late into the night, I got up early in the morning and studied. I studied during load shedding in the night, every day, for at least four hours under an oil lamp with a wick. My father asked me to take a break during the load shedding, but I did not listen to him. It came to a point when I lost my eyes, when one afternoon I saw darkness before my eyes. My father immediately took me to an optometrist. I was given thick glasses to wear and I became the bespectacled boy, which in popular language is called the 'perfect' geek. I did not stop and carried on with my struggle.

The exams came and I wrote all that I had studied and tried to grasp.

Fast forward the results came out. I scored 80% each in Hindi, Social Science (History, Geography and Civics), a 92% in science, 52% in English, 69% in Computer Science (a fairly new subject, then) and finally an 80% in Mathematics.

People around me congratulated me on the good performance, including firstly by my happy parents, and I always thought the papers were easy and that my performance was not all that exceptional, without trying to fake my feelings which were true.

I did not see Ms. Bedi, my class teacher at all. She was surrounded, I guess, by students that had scored 97% over all. I was just a small fish.

That partially ended the misery that Mathematics had caused me. I am happy to report that after I got admission in Bihar College of Engineering, Patna (now NIT, Patna) in the Mechanical Engineering, I did very well in a paper called 'Engineering Mathematics'.

I finally admit that I am no Mathematician, I am more of a broke artist that lives on poetry and music.

The real geniuses in Mathematics, perhaps are people that dream of numbers in their sleep. I have proclaimed too many times to myself and others, that I am very weak in Mathematics. It is sad what people can do to you, by forcefully making you believe that you have no hold over the subject. They will try to put you down by doing some swift calculations in a fast conversation, thus showing you how weak you are in the subject. The fact is that they had already known the answers before they engaged with you in a conversation. This is nothing but fraud, cheating, and it sadly effects young children the most. It is true that people like me are then discouraged to even try to do some calculations on their own and figure out the answers. It is true that the world is made up of people that are glib and carry masks to hide their poverty. A truly intelligent man is one that carries a halo of silence and patient listening, and would never utter a word to lower the dignity of the other person and would happily wear the mantle of a fool if so required.

Misery is within a person,
That cannot be hidden or done for,
For those that have never heard,
The sound of rumbling earth,

Shall never know the depth of intelligence,
Nor the flight of the human heart,
Shall never know 'human',
For there are kingdoms the exist,
With no spoken word.'

CHAPTER SEVEN

THE MEAGRE SCHOOL

I was thirteen years old when we (family of four) arrived at Patna. It was an impossible place for us and the first time that we tasted civilian life, at least my brother and me. We were living an easy life of comforts in the laps of the Air Force stations. When my father took a premature retirement and decided to move from New Delhi to Patna, all eyes turned to him with a question that my father got used to hearing – 'Why in the world can you decide to retire and worst of all choose to go to Patna for the rest of your life.'

My father probably did not have clear answers but only the fact that he was suffering from hypertension and did not want to be admitted to hospitals as a military procedure each time his blood pressure shot up. There was a deep mystery in the step that he took and a sick body did not suffice for his sudden step completely. Yet my father being an altruistic person all his life had others welfare on his mind in whatever he did. Why then did he spend many sleepless nights sitting by the side of the bed with someone close that was sick and the doctor prescribed a round the clock monitor of the sick one. This is just a whiff of what my father was all about and the lengths to which he went in the service of others. Probably my father got a purpose to live when his two children were born. This was a man who had seen the darkness of the night and the sun rise eventually through his heavy eyes umpteen times and pleaded before God to take him away if there was nothing left to do. At the arrival of his children, he was in the Indian Airforce as a flying officer. Life just carried on and the birth of children is not an unusual event when most of what is born is trash. He never had any hopes for his children for he knew that life is nothing but a sacrifice and the pain that a human can bear without filching. This is a war of truth and the liars have no place here. He was taken aback once when his younger son, a baby then, became acutely sick. Once he was travelling on a train with his wife and two children. The elder one was a young child and the younger one was a baby in his mother's arms. Mid way through the journey the baby got seriously sick. His whole body was swollen from some kind of allergy. He was extremely serious and my father started panicking. He got up from his seat and told my mother that he as going to search for a doctor. He walked and walked, shouting out for any doctor until he reached the very end of the train in one direction. There was no doctor anywhere. He walked back and this time took the opposite direction where the majority of the bogeys lay. He walked and walked until he reached the engine. There was no doctor. In great frustration he walked back thinking that he was going to lose his baby. As a lifeless body he reached his seat to find a doctor attending to his baby,

"Mr. Srivastava, don't you have a heart. This baby will die, how could you take him on a train and travel. You cannot be so careless. Please, this baby needs a hospital. Get down in the next stop and rush to a hospital or you shall lose this baby."

The baby was serious and my father got down on the next stop and luckily, he knew where the hospital was for the place where he alighted the train was very near his actual destination. My father closed his eyes and the baby was rushed and finally reached a secure bed in a hospital. By that time the baby's condition was even more serious and it would not have been a surprise if he heard that the baby did not make it. He and my mother waited for hours until the doctor came out and when my father touched his cold hands, the doctor said,

"The baby has survived. He is fine. The swelling will go away in a few days. Relax Mr. Srivastava."

That day my father's outlook towards his children changed completely. This younger son of his fought very hard for his life and eventually came out from the jaws of death. My father decided to devote the rest of his life to his children as there was some hope somewhere, after all.

When my father decided to go to Patna, then, it was well known why he was doing it and the mystery was unlocked, may be by mother too, but no one else at all.

My brother and me got admission in Don Bosco Academy, one the best schools in the city. A little recommendation from someone that knew the principal was the decider and we soon started classes. It was a meagre school that did not even have a building of its own at the time. Our school existed in rented houses that were three in number. In my three years at the school until I gave the tenth board exams, I attended classes in all the three buildings with the final one being the main building. I was surprised and in disbelief at the arrangements having attended schools with huge buildings of their own. Moreover, the teachers surprised me the most. There was a huge number of Keralite teachers and their English was beyond atrocious. We Indians speak Hindi or many other local languages all across India. In the Devanagari script for example the words are spoken just they way they are written or spelt. But that's not true of English where silence is one of the alphabets and must be spoken or unspoken when required or else, we end up making a mess of our pronunciation. Hence Knowledge is not *Cnolej* but *Nolej*, dysentery is not *dysentri* but *disentri*, situation is not *syntuatian* but *situashun*, vendor is not *ven...door* but *vendur* and the list is too big. Such was the atrocity towards English language, especially by those Keralite teachers but the sweat on their forehead said something else. The school might have been cramped for space but I can never forget the effort that each teacher made to go deep into the subject. The force of dedication and total submission to the text at hand was exemplary. I might have complained somewhere I am sure looking at what I saw around me - the dearth of benches, blackboards, chalk, the poverty of the teachers, lack of space, the strong smell of sweat and grime, the low crowd, the level of English, the lack of playgrounds, etc. But I don't know why I always wanted to forget everything and look into the eyes of those teachers that would not leave a word in the text without an expression of it. This was the first school where a seriousness towards education began. My father did realize it also. For the first time he saw his children opening their books at home and trying to understand what was written in them. The teachers tried their best to invite students into the world of books and knowledge by breaking and simplifying the study material like reading the English alphabet. I found it increasingly encouraging to dive into those books to say the least and discovered that studying was fun and easy. A meagre school was thus the best in the city and better than those that could afford a huge building and facilities bent on entertainment more than anything else. But this was a skeletal of a school and promised great things in the form of new learnings. The teachers were very encouraging and behaved more like friends, passing on the usual invective if required. The star of the show was our Physics teacher by the name of Mr. Donald Martin. Everyone loved him and hated him the most. I have never seen a man with such passion for his subject. He literally shouted in the class and explained each word in the book with great thrust with a strained face to the point of spitting clarity. It felt like he was about to have a heart attack, or his vocal cord were about to give in. If there was someone that was not paying attention, he carried on with his vocals and simultaneously threw a piece of chalk at the culprit and if he was forced to stop abruptly, it didn't matter if you were the son of the king of Nepal, he just swore and cussed, lending all such dirty words he knew, some to the extent of a mumble that was fully understood by the boys of the class. This is the land of Bihar, do not expect softness or kindness here, you will get all the dirt and the filth that you can never imagine. Such was the policy of the great Don Bosco Academy and teachers lived and died each day at office in the heat and the dust that floated around. Do not look at what they wear or how they look, pay attention or else you shall be blown away in the storm. Mr. Donald Martin did not shy away from giving his all to the students and by his perfect handwriting on the blackboard and his slow and cautious move through each word, each sentence like the greatest mystery of the world was hidden in those words. His English was perfect and he just knew how to tackle big boys and bad boys and nothing boys just by the flick of his tongue. I regard him as the greatest teacher that I came across in my entire career at school. He was tall, handsome, impressive in all possible ways and at my age I knew nothing of married or not married and I later guessed that he might have been married at that time.

It happened once when I was in the eighth grade. We had our regular terminal exams and that was a period of seriousness like in a funeral and we were expected to pass all the papers. There was a constant danger that I may not be promoted to the ninth grade and this fear of mine was shared by my group of mediocre and below mediocre students. The toppers took the terminal exams as a opportunity to show how brilliant they were and push the mediocre and below mediocre in a deep well of shame and face the might of darkness and death. I was very upset and worried and thought that I was not good enough to be promoted and that my fuel that is stored in the brain was running out fast. I was behaving like a sixty-five-year-old, slow and lost. The terminal exams were held in the right manner with the eyes of the invigilators on the students like the eagles that sore in the skies with a keen eye on the ground and any attempt to cheat would result in the immediate wrath and final expulsion from the school. Then you could go home where you father would gently inform you,

"Thanks for your auspicious company. You are done staying with us, please leave, take your things and don't you ever show your face again."

These are just some of the fears that are faced by twelve- or thirteen-year-olds while the rest of the world is just not bothered what kind of fish you are and school is like a wasted life. We attended classes after the exam and the results slowly started seeping through even before the final report card was to be distributed among the students in the presence of the parents. One by one I passed in all the papers except physics. I got thirty-eight out of hundred when the passing mark was forty out of hundred. I thought that was the end of the world. That day Mr. Donald Martin gave out the marks of the terminal exams. Toppers just smirked and looked around to make some ordinary student feel low and inferior. I just could not believe that I missed the mark by just two marks. I was in tears and I ran to Mr. Donald Martin as he was making his way out of the classroom after distributing the marks. I went to his and begged,

"Please sir, some grace marks. I have failed and I am greatly upset and worried that I may not make to the next grade."

Mr. Donald Martin looked at me and touched my shoulder,

"Do not worry son. It's Ok and just to tell you that I do not give any grace marks. Hold yourself please, all will be fine."

I cried softly and when I found others laughing and jumping around, even those in the mediocre and below mediocre category, I just forgot about crying and carried a serious face and could not be amused by anything at all.

Such were the teachers of Don Bosco Academy. Well, I was never denied promotion and never got more than a grave face and stern warning from my teachers at the Parent Teacher's meet. I progressed from one rented house to another until the time arrived to announce the birth of youth at sixteen in the tenth grade in building number 152. This was the main building where we had too much of brilliance under one roof while I continued with my infamous mediocre group. My class teacher one Ms. Bedi was a cruel woman, a strict teacher. She warned my father of severe consequences if I did not work hard and the future could be brighter if only I could manage a miracle somewhere. Shashank Shekhar was the emerging genius that the entire school witnessed. He started getting noticed when he reached ninth grade. This boy was special and through his efforts he managed to top the class in the ninth grade. I could see him scribbling on his notebook in the entire time that he sat in the class. Even when it was a free period and rest of the boys were busy making noise and trying to disrupt the class like a 'strike' and did not like the school or its teachers and the management, this tall boy wrote and wrote sitting on his bench endlessly. He never stood second after his emergence and it is said that he beat the topper of many years in the tenth board exams. We just looked at ourselves and wondered how these geniuses managed such feats while we could not get the question right in our brains in the exams. Each of the mediocre and below mediocre students had their own lame excuse and mine looked like the most genuine- how can you concentrate in a house where there are turbulent waves of mayhem and disorder with my father suffering from hypertension. It meant that he managed to create a ruckus every living moment by creating a mountain out of a mole hill. Today I would say that even that was a lame excuse that I made and it's not right to give someone a crown of thorns for our own shortcomings and failures. However, I did give my all in the tenth board exams to the extent of losing my eyes and becoming this bespectacled geek. I took to my books even in the evenings and nights when there was a power failure and the flame of the lamp was all that I had to figure out the letters and sentences of my books. My father just stopped me sometimes and asked me to wait for power to be restored, even if I had not read enough for my next exam. In my board exams I managed to get ninety-two percent in science with a ninety seven percent in biology. Even today my brother reminds me of the ninety-two percent, which is higher than what he got in his board exams and I simply say that it was an easy exam and did not really test the students. But an eighty precent in mathematics did surprise me, for a boy that would often cry at the dinner table because he could not solve a mathematical puzzle tossed at him by his father and his brother just jumped at such occasions to show me how stupid I was, by solving it like 'a, b, c'.

It's hard to understand the mechanics of this world and where each individual stands in the scheme of this world. Success and failure are an illusory concept and the last word in this world is perhaps summed up in the two beautiful lines of the Robert Frost Poem '*Stopping by Woods on a Snowy Evening*',

'*...But I have promises to keep,*
And miles to go before I sleep...'

Life thus is not a one-day affair, it lasts for centuries/ages and if someone wants to get it right then he better stop and think where he is headed. If then, it comes easy and rainbows make you sick and the rain is a disaster, you probably are on the wrong path. It often looks like the world is headed towards the lighter path,

'*...The woods are lovely, dark and deep...*' (Robert Frost)

Do not ask if people are lost and where each new face reminds us of a new religion. Hence the truth is not what we hear aloud in heavy decibels across the streets and into the villages, celebrating success like it were easy as apple pie. Pain is the only redemption and it comes as no surprise when we get mistaken by a person's gentility, persona or the exquisite way of one's dress. It is a great road ahead and it takes an eternity to understand people and what goes on around us, unfelt and unheard. And we all catch on to that phrase of the great cliched philosophy – '*Life is too short*'.

That meagre school and its teachers have been forgotten in the common folklore. Students that emerged in that period have had great success in life and some have even become world famous. There is nothing one can give to others if there is nothing of substance within us. Those teachers of Don Bosco Academy toiled hard each day in a school that was not yet a school. Their voices loud and clear, like the great force of an unsettled sea trying to get somewhere. What happened was very much normal when good work is not without reverses, obstacles and sometimes unruly children totally disrupted the learning process by passing some objectionable comments that was hard to bear by the teachers. There was some element of truth in the eyes of all those teachers that made the students eventually give up their frivolity and join in a great mission. Those teachers changed the lives of many students completely and gave them the strong foundation on which they could build their fortress of dreams. Students emerged with immaculate English or sound knowledge of basics of science and mathematics and that later reached the best colleges around the country. I realized that it is not the command over the subject itself that makes a great teacher or a school. It is the relentless efforts of the teachers each day as the morning assembly dispersed and each teacher entered his/her war room to delineate a point that truth, passion, sincerity, honesty, hard work are the pillars that make a great human being and the marks obtained in exams is no measure of an individual. I heard Mr. Donald Martin when he saw tears in my eyes and a certain history teacher by the name of Mr. Arvind Shah that once touched my shoulder when I sat in some school exam, lost and defeated, telling me that all is not lost.

I still remember those teachers like true warriors, ready to face...

'My little horse must think it queer

To stop without a farmhouse near

Between the woods and frozen lake

The darkest evening of the year.' (Robert Frost again)

For it is from the dark that rises the light. Why can't we be brave and face the dark even if it lasts forever, just like those dedicated teachers of that meagre school, my alma mater, Don Bosco Academy.